This book is for Sir Henry Moore,
who loves to draw sheep
from his studio window…
and with special thanks to
Nicole Sekora, who almost
became a rhyme.

Silly Sheep
and Other Sheepish Rhymes

Selected by George Mendoza
Illustrated by Kathleen Reidy

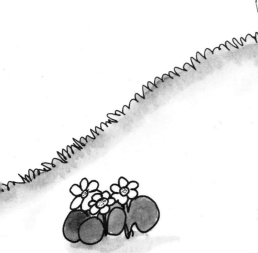

Publishers • GROSSET & DUNLAP • New York

Library of Congress Catalog Card Number: 82-81045. ISBN: 0-448-12219-7.
Text copyright © 1982 by Ruth Sekora. Illustrations copyright © 1982 by Kathleen Reidy.

May we introduce ourselves,
May we say hello, hello?
You will surely love us all—
If you come and see our show.

Call us silly, call us sheep,
Acting out each game and rhyme.
Do stop by and visit us—
We'll have a grand old time.

Our shepherd also greets you,
With his woolly dog called Rife.
He's our very own director—
Watch him bring each rhyme to life!

Act VI

"Hello, hello, hello, sir,
Meet me at the grocer."
"No sir."
"Why sir?"
"Because I have a cold, sir."
"Where did you get your cold, sir?"
"At the North Pole, sir."
"What were you doing there, sir?"
"Shooting polar bear, sir."
"Let me hear you sneeze, sir."
"Kachoo, kachoo, kachoo, sir."

I like coffee, I like tea,
I like the boys and the boys like me.
Tell your mother to hold her tongue,
For she did the same when she was young.
Tell your father to do the same,
For he was the one who changed her name.

I had a little lamb,
 The prettiest ever seen;

She washed up the dishes,
 And kept the house clean.

She went to the mill
 To fetch me some flour,

And always got home
In less than an hour.

She baked me my bread,
She brewed me my ale,

She sat by the fire
And told a fine tale.

Little Sally Water,
Sitting in a saucer;

Rise, Sally, rise,
Wipe off your eyes.

Put your hand on your hip;
Don't let your backbone slip.

Turn to the East, Sally,
Turn to the West,

Turn to the one, Sally,
That you love the best.

Paddy O'Flynn had no breeches to wear,
So they bought him a sheepskin and made him a pair,
The woolly side out and the skinny side in—
They made very good breeches for Paddy O'Flynn.

Little Boy Blue,
    Come blow your horn!
The sheep's in the meadow,
    The cow's in the corn.
Where is the boy
    Who looks after the sheep?
He's under the haystack,
    Fast asleep.
Will you wake him?
    No, not I.
For if I do,
    He'll be sure to cry.

Old shepherd, old shepherd, my kind man,
Shear me some wool as fast as you can;

Spin it and weave it, and mark it to me,

Send it quickly SPECIAL DELIVERY!

Tit for tat,
Butter for fat;
If you kick my dog,
I'll kick your cat.

There she goes! There she goes!
All dressed up in her Sunday clothes.

Open your mouth and shut your eyes;
I'll give you something to make you wise.

London Bridge is falling down,
Falling down, falling down;
London Bridge is falling down,
My fair lady.
I caught one, I caught two,
I caught many, and I caught you.

Eenie, meenie, minie, mo,
Catch a tiger by the toe,
If he hollers let him go,
Eenie, meenie, minie, mo.

Eenie, meenie, minie, mo.
Catch a thief by the toe;
If he hollers make him pay
Fifty dollars every day.

The sheep go marching in a line,
    Hurrah! Hurrah!
The sheep go marching three, six, nine,
    Hurrah! Hurrah!

The sheep go marching rum-tum-tum,
The little one stops to tap his drum,
And they all go marching down
   And around
   And around
   And down.

Here we go round the mulberry bush,
The mulberry bush, the mulberry bush,
Here we go round the mulberry bush,
On a cold and frosty morning.

Little lamb, little lamb, turn around,
Little lamb, little lamb, touch the ground.
Little lamb, little lamb, jump up high,
Little lamb, little lamb, reach the sky.
Little lamb, little lamb, do not miss,
Little lamb, little lamb, skip like this.
Little lamb, little lamb, out you go,
Little lamb, little lamb, don't be slow.

A sheep and a goat were going to the pasture.
Said the goat to the sheep, "Can't you walk a little faster?"
The sheep said, "I can't. I'm a little too full."
The goat said, "You could with my horns in your wool."
But the goat fell down and skinned his shin,
And the sheep split his lip with a big wide grin.

Little Bo-Peep has lost her sheep,
And can't tell where to find them;
Leave them alone, and they'll come home,
And bring their tails behind them.

Little Bo-Peep fell fast asleep,
And dreamt she heard them bleating;
And when she awoke she found it a joke,
For still they all were fleeting.

Then up she took her little crook,
Determined for to find them;
She found them, indeed, but it made her heart bleed,
For they'd left all their tails behind them.

It happened one day, as Bo-Peep did stray
Into the meadow hard by,
There she espied their tails side by side,
All hung on a tree to dry.

She heaved a sigh, and wiped her eye,
Then went o'er hill and dale, oh;
And tried what she could, as a shepherdess should,
To tack to each sheep its tail, oh.

Bushel of wheat, bushel of barley,
All not hid, holler "Charley."

Bushel of wheat, bushel of rye,
All not hid, holler "I."

Bushel of wheat, bushel of clover,
All not hid, can't hide over.
All eyes open! Here I come.

Old King Cole,
Was a merry old soul,
And a merry old soul was he;
And he called for his pipe,
And he called for his glass,
And he called for his fiddlers three.

And every fiddler, he had a fine fiddle,
And a very fine fiddle had he;
"Twee tweedle dee, tweedle dee," went the fiddlers.
Oh there's none so rare
As can compare
With King Cole and his fiddlers three.

Anna Banana
Played the piano;
The piano broke
And Anna choked.

Margaret, Margaret, has big eyes,
Spread all over the skies.

Jane, Jane,
The window pane.

Sally bum-bally
Tee-ally go fally
Tee-legged, tie-legged
Bow-legged Sally.

Mary, Mary, don't say no,
Or into the closet you must go.

Rose, Rose,
Has big toes;
She carries them
Wherever she goes.

Mary had a little lamb,
   Its fleece was white as snow;
And everywhere that Mary went,
   The lamb was sure to go.

He followed her to school one day,
   That was against the rule;
It made the children laugh and play,
   To see the lamb at school.

So the teacher turned him out,
   But still he lingered near;
And waited patiently about,
   Till Mary did appear.

Then he ran to her, and laid
   His head upon her arm,
As if he said, "I'm not afraid,
   You'll keep me from all harm!"

"What makes the lamb love Mary so?"
   The eager children cry;
"Oh, Mary loves the lamb, you know,"
   The teacher did reply.

Dance to your daddy,
My little baby,
Dance to your daddy,
My little lamb.
You shall have a fishy
In a little dishy,
You shall have a fishy
When the boat comes in.

Shepherdess Shire sheared a shaggy sheep;
A shaggy sheep Shepherdess Shire sheared;
If Shepherdess Shire sheared a shaggy sheep,
Where is the shorn sheep Shepherdess Shire shore?

Baa, baa, black sheep,
    Have you any wool?
Yes, sir, yes, sir,
    Three bags full:
One for my master,
    One for my dame,
And one for the little boy
    Who lives in our lane.

I should worry, I should care,
I should marry a millionaire;
He should die, I should cry—
Then I'd marry a richer guy.

Roses are red,
Violets are blue,
What you need
Is a good shampoo

When you get married
And your husband gets cross,
Pick up the broom
And say, "I'm boss!"

Cry, baby, cry,
Stick your finger in your eye;
If your mother asks you why,
Tell her that you want some pie.

The shepherd went up the hill
To find his lost sheep,
And what do you think he saw?

He saw another hill,
and what do you think he did?

He climbed that other hill
To find his lost sheep,
And what do you think he saw?

He saw another hill,
and what do you think he did?

He climbed that other hill
To find his...

Ten little shearlings marching in a line,
One got lost and then there were nine;

Nine little shearlings staying out too late,
One got sleepy and then there were eight.

Eight little shearlings frolicking through Devon,
One got sheared and then there were seven;

Seven little shearlings jumping over sticks,
One got wobbly and then there were six.

Six little shearlings poking at a hive,
One got chased and then there were five;

Five little shearlings bleating at the door,
One got inside and then there were four.

Four little shearlings looking out to sea,
One got sickly and then there were three;

Three little shearlings listening to owls whooo,
One got frightened and then there were two.

Two little shearlings romping in the sun,
One got dizzy and then there was one;

One little shearling standing all alone,
He toddled off home and then there were none.